DEREK JETER

A Real-Life Reader Biography

John Torres

Mitchell Lane Publishers, Inc.
P.O. Box 619 • Bear, Delaware 19701

Copyright © 2001 by Mitchell Lane Publishers. All rights reserved. No part of this book may be reproduced without written permission from the publisher. Printed and bound in the United States of America.

Second Printing
Real-Life Reader Biographies

Paula Abdul	Mary Joe Fernandez	Ricky Martin	Arnold Schwarzenegger
Christina Aguilera	Andres Galarraga	Mark McGwire	Selena
Marc Anthony	Sarah Michelle Gellar	Alyssa Milano	Maurice Sendak
Drew Barrymore	Jeff Gordon	Mandy Moore	Dr. Seuss
Brandy	Mia Hamm	Chuck Norris	Shakira
Garth Brooks	Melissa Joan Hart	Tommy Nuñez	Alicia Silverstone
Kobe Bryant	Jennifer Love Hewitt	Rosie O'Donnell	Jessica Simpson
Sandra Bullock	Faith Hill	Rafael Palmeiro	Sinbad
Mariah Carey	Hollywood Hogan	Gary Paulsen	Jimmy Smits
Cesar Chavez	Katie Holmes	Freddie Prinze, Jr.	Sammy Sosa
Christopher Paul Curtis	Enrique Iglesias	Julia Roberts	Britney Spears
Roald Dahl	**Derek Jeter**	Robert Rodriguez	Sheryl Swoopes
Oscar De La Hoya	Steve Jobs	J.K. Rowling	Shania Twain
Trent Dimas	Michelle Kwan	Keri Russell	Liv Tyler
Celine Dion	Bruce Lee	Winona Ryder	Robin Williams
Sheila E.	Jennifer Lopez	Cristina Saralegui	Vanessa Williams
Gloria Estefan	Cheech Marin		Tiger Woods

Library of Congress Cataloging-in-Publication Data
Torres, John Albert.
    Derek Jeter/John Torres.
       p. cm. — (A real-life reader biography)
    Includes index.
    Summary: A biography of the premier shortstop who helped lead the New York Yankees to three World Series championships in the 1990's.
      ISBN 1-58415-031-9
    1. Jeter, Derek, 1974—Juvenile literature. 2. Baseball players—United States—Biography—Juvenile Literature.
    [1. Jeter, Derek, 1974- 2. Baseball players. 3. Racially mixed people—Biography.] I. Title. II. Series.
GV865.J48 T67 2001
796.357'092—dc21
[B]
                                                                                                                                                                                       00-027047

ABOUT THE AUTHOR: John A. Torres is a newspaper reporter for the Poughkeepsie Journal in New York. He has written eleven sports biographies, including *Greg Maddux* (Lerner), *Hakeem Olajuwon* (Enslow), and *Darryl Strawberry* (Enslow). He lives in Fishkill, New York with his wife and two children. When not writing, John likes to spend his time fishing, coaching Little League baseball, and spending time with his family.
PHOTO CREDITS: Cover: Otto Greule/Allsport ; p. 4 Reuters/Mike Segar/Archive Photos; p. 6; F. Newman Lowrance/The Sporting Image; p. 7 Corbis/Mitch Gerber; p. 10 Kirby Lee/The Sporting Image; p. 14 Reuters/Winston Luzier/Archive Photos; p. 20 Kirby Lee/The Sporting Image; p. 23 G. Newman Lowrance/The Sporting Image; p. 24 Doug Pensinger/Allsport; p. 27 John M. Mantel/Corbis; p. 29 John Barrett/Globe Photos; p. 30 Jamie Squire/Allsport.
ACKNOWLEDGMENTS: The following story has been thoroughly researched, and to the best of our knowledge, represents a true story. While every possible effort has been made to ensure accuracy, the publisher will not assume liability for damages caused by inaccuracies in the data, and makes no warranty on the accuracy of the information contained herein.

Table of Contents

Chapter 1 Setting Standards 5

Chapter 2 Yankees Fan 9

Chapter 3 Diamond in the Rough 13

Chapter 4 Gaining Confidence 18

Chapter 5 Learning From the Pros 22

Chapter 6 Rookie of the Year 26

Chapter 7 A Perfect Match 28

Major-League Stats 31

Chronology 32

Index 32

Chapter 1
Setting Standards

Veteran baseball scout Dick Groch had spent his life watching young baseball players. He had already seen thousands of ballplayers by the time he found himself watching a high-school baseball game in Flint, Michigan.

Groch could not believe his eyes. He stared as a tall, skinny shortstop scooped up every ground ball hit his way and then fired them to first base. Breathless, he watched the high-school sophomore named Derek Jeter.

During the next two years, Groch spent a lot of time following the youngster and telling many of the other scouts

> He stared as a tall, skinny shortstop scooped up every ground ball hit his way.

Derek has always been a talented baseball player.

and officials within the New York Yankees organization about Derek. By the time Derek was a high-school senior, Groch had convinced the Yankees that they should take him with their first pick of the 1992 draft.

"A player like this makes you hyperventilate," Groch said. "There's only one place Derek Jeter's going for sure: the Hall of Fame."

Those are bold words about a kid who had never played one inning of professional baseball, but Groch was sure of what many would soon know: Derek Jeter was a great baseball player.

Just a few years later, Derek Jeter would be a key player on one of the greatest baseball teams of all time. In 1996, as a rookie, he experienced the ultimate as the starting shortstop for a championship team. He was rewarded with a World Series ring and a Rookie of the Year award. In 1998 he finished third in the American League Most Valuable Player voting as he helped the Yankees win their second World Series of the 1990s. A year later, he simply dominated baseball again with his speed, power, agility, and great fielding to help the Yankees win their third championship in three years. In fact, it is hard to find a baseball player who is capable of putting up the same impressive numbers as Derek is. In 1999 he belted 24 home runs, drove in 102 runs, and hit better than .340. All those numbers show an improvement from 1998 when he first began to glimmer as a superstar.

Derek takes time to sign autographs for his fans.

> **Most baseball experts agree that Derek is still nowhere near reaching his full potential.**

Most baseball experts agree that Derek is still nowhere near reaching his full potential. That is a scary thought for opposing pitchers who have a hard time figuring out how to strike out the young player. His body is getting bigger and stronger, and Derek continues to work on his game, trying to become the best player he possibly can be.

Derek is an all-star not only on the baseball field. Just about everyone who comes in contact with him agrees that he is one of the nicest people they have ever met.

"He's the kind of guy you hope your son can grow up to be," said Derek's Yankee teammate Darryl Strawberry. "Derek has a great deal of respect for everyone he encounters. That's what sets him apart."

But somehow, Derek always hoped that he would end up being a baseball star for the Yankees, his favorite team.

Chapter 2
Yankees Fan

Derek Sanderson Jeter was born on June 26, 1974, in Pequannock, New Jersey. While he was still young, his family moved north to Kalamazoo, Michigan.

His father, Charles, moved the family there so that he could take a job as a clinical therapist specializing in drug and alcohol counseling. He liked helping people who needed and wanted to be helped. Derek's mother, Dorothy, found a job as a credit manager.

Charles is an African-American who was born in Alabama. Dorothy is white, from Irish ancestry, and was born in New Jersey. Derek was lucky enough

> **Derek's father helped people who needed and wanted to be helped.**

Derek spent all his time playing sports when he was young.

to grow up in an environment where he learned about both cultures.

"A lot of people think I'm Hispanic," Derek said. "My upbringing was a lot like *The Cosby Show*. We had fun and always did a lot of things together. My parents were involved in everything my sister and I did."

From a young age, Derek showed that he was very athletic. He would spend just about all his free time playing baseball, basketball, and football with his friends.

He starred in Little League, where, even though he was always one of the skinnier players, he had a knack for hitting the baseball. His father said that during his Little League years, Derek used to repeat something that ended up coming true.

"When he was in Little League, he said that he was going to play for the Yankees someday," Charles Jeter said. "He's been saying that for a long time. It's amazing that the Yankees drafted him in the first round."

When he was a child, Derek often came back to the East Coast. He spent his summer vacations at his grandparents' house in northern New Jersey. In the evenings he watched the New York Yankees play baseball on television. That is how he became such a big Yankees fan. His favorite player was Dave Winfield. Derek loved the way that Winfield always played as hard as he could. He liked Winfield even more

> "When he was in Little League, he said that he was going to play for the Yankees someday."

when he found out that he was involved in a lot of charity work.

Back home in Michigan, Derek and his sister, Sharlee, would sometimes get teased about their multiracial background. Some kids would say mean things to them about having a black father and a white mother.

"People sometimes said things, but my feeling was always, why let an ignorant person bother me?" Derek said. "Growing up, I had friends who were black, white, and Hispanic. I was always surrounded by so many good people. My parents, I'm sure, had to deal with it a lot more than I did. They all made it easy for me."

Derek's parents made it easy for him and his sister by sometimes making things hard. They provided their children with a lot of love and affection, but they also made sure that their strict rules were followed.

> **Derek and his sister would sometimes get teased about their multiracial background.**

Chapter 3
Diamond in the Rough

Every year before school started, Charles and Dorothy would sit down with Derek and Sharlee and set certain ground rules. They would then make the children sign a written contract promising to keep up their end of the bargain.

The contract was always very specific and dealt with many things such as study habits, chores, curfew, and a promise never to take drugs or alcohol. The kids were expected to maintain an A average in school as well as keep current with chores.

Derek and his sister were expected to maintain an A average in school.

Derek is considered an all-around good guy by his friends.

Derek never had a problem with the agreement, but it sometimes bothered his sister.

"I always tried to negotiate," Sharlee said with a laugh. "But Derek just sat there and nodded. It was hard having this older brother who did everything he was supposed to do."

Derek would do everything that was expected of him and dreamt of playing for the Yankees. Sometimes he would stand in his bedroom and hold a baseball bat while staring at the Dave Winfield poster on his wall. He would go into his stance and pretend to hit long home runs like his idol. But Derek had two dreams. One, of course, was to be a Yankee. The second was to follow in his father's footsteps and help others.

Charles was a good baseball player as well. Like Derek, he played shortstop. Charles even hit a home run in his first college baseball game. He was not good enough to make the major leagues, however, and he decided to dedicate himself to helping people stay away from drugs and alcohol.

As Derek entered his teenage years, he was very shy. His parents were concerned and tried to get him involved in activities with other children his age.

"When he was 12 or 13, I took him to a basketball camp at the University of Michigan," said his father. "When it came time for him to meet the other

As Derek entered his teenage years, he was very shy.

15

kids, I had to push him to make conversation."

Part of Derek's shyness probably stemmed from the fact that after the eighth grade he switched from a parochial school to a public school. He was nervous about the change, and about making new friends.

Aside from the shyness, Derek made the transition to the new high school without much of a hitch. He fit in right away, especially when he got on the baseball field. His new friends also liked his easygoing style. Derek was the kind of person who did not get upset easily. He was a genuinely nice person, and other kids just seemed to gravitate toward him.

Derek grew a lot more serious about baseball after finally getting to Yankee Stadium during one of his visits to his grandparents' home. He was in awe of the big, beautiful field. He hoped that one day he would get a chance to play on the green grass of the infield.

> **Derek was the kind of person who did not get upset easily.**

Derek grew several inches in high school and soon was a dominating force at shortstop. That's when he was first spotted by the Yankee scout who knew he had discovered a diamond in the rough.

Chapter 4
Gaining Confidence

Michigan's cold weather only allows for a certain number of games each year.

Growing up in Michigan is not easy for young baseball players. The harsh weather allows for only a certain number of games between the last thaw of spring and the first snowfall the next winter.

Traditionally, warm-weather states like Florida and California produce the highest numbers of professional baseball players. As youngsters, children from warm-climate states have the edge of being able to play baseball year-round. Many of the amateur and youth leagues play baseball in the fall and spring as well. Even though he was a tremendously gifted athlete, and even though he was a great high-school baseball player, Derek had not played in nearly the amount of baseball games that other kids his age had.

During his senior year of high school, Derek signed a letter of intent to attend the University of Michigan. But the Yankees were confident that he would skip college if they drafted him as their first-round pick. They were right.

When the Yankees drafted Derek, he was assigned to New York's rookie-league team in Tampa Bay, Florida. Derek did not adjust well. He had a hard time on the playing field, and he had a hard time being away from his family.

"I cried in my room every night," he said. "I'd never been away from home before. I didn't feel like I belonged. I felt overmatched."

In 47 rookie-league games, Derek batted a paltry .202 and struck out once every five times he came to the plate.

> Derek did not adjust well to New York's rookie-league team in Tampa Bay.

Although Derek didn't perform well in the rookie-leagues, the Yankees knew he could play.

But still the Yankees promoted him to Class-A Greensboro for the final two weeks of the season. Even though Derek had not performed well, the Yankees felt it was vital to show Derek that they had faith in him.

Yankees catcher Jorge Posada was a teammate of Derek's at Greensboro. He remembers seeing Derek for the first time and not being overly impressed—until Derek took the field.

"His shirt and pants were too big," Posada said. "He didn't know how to wear a hat. He looked like a Little Leaguer."

But after watching Derek snare hard-hit grounders up the middle game after game, and after watching him slam the baseball into the outfield gaps, driving in runners, Posada changed his mind.

"He could play," he said. "There was no doubt about it."

Derek finished strong at Greensboro, and the toughest year of his life was under his belt. After the season, Derek went back home to Michigan. He was happy to be there.

After enjoying a winter with his family, Derek was invited to the big-league spring training camp. It was something that the Yankee organization did with all its first-round picks. It was a way of making these young players feel special.

Many people would have been intimidated by having to share a baseball field with some of the all-time great baseball players like Don Mattingly and Wade Boggs. But Derek was not intimidated in the least. In fact, being near them gave him the confidence he needed.

"I saw that I had the ability to make it," Derek said. "I also knew how hard I would have to work."

Being near great baseball players like Don Mattingly and Wade Boggs gave Derek the confidence he needed.

Chapter 5
Learning From the Pros

> "We had better run off the field," Mattingly said. "You never know who is watching."

That first spring training, when Derek Jeter seemed like just a kid playing baseball alongside legends, he learned a lesson that he would never forget. It was late afternoon in the hot Florida sun and the Yankees had just finished a grueling workout.

Derek and superstar Don Mattingly were the last two Yankees on the field. They began walking off together.

"We had better run off the field," Mattingly told the youngster. "You never know who is watching."

Derek looked around and did not see anybody. He stopped in his tracks and let Mattingly's words sink in. All he could think about was, 'Here is Don Mattingly, one of the all-time greatest Yankee players, and even he doesn't let himself walk off the field.'

Derek is now one of the Yankees' biggest stars.

"There were no fans, no coaches, no media around. Nobody was watching," Derek said. "That made a big impression on me. Since that day, when I'm on the field, I always run. I'll never forget that story."

By the end of 1994, with major-league players on strike, Derek had moved up to the Yankees Triple-A team in Columbus,

Derek helped the New York Yankees reach the World Series in 1998. He is not only a good hitter, but an excellent outfielder as well.

Ohio. He had his old confidence back and was tearing up the minor-league pitching.

In 1995 Derek went to spring training as a bonafide top prospect with a real chance to make the team. But he was still very young, and the Yankees wanted him to have another full season in the minor leagues. Besides, the Yankees had a pretty good full-time shortstop in Kevin Elster.

But Elster started the season poorly and was sent down to the minors. Derek was called up on May 29 and spent three full weeks with the major-league club. He played well, but he was sent back down on June 12. The Yankees knew that Derek was not yet ready to be a full-time major-leaguer, and they wanted him to get as much playing time as he could in the minor leagues.

It turned out to be a good move. In 123 games at Columbus, Derek batted .317, drove in 45 runs, and stole 20 bases. He also led the league with 96 runs scored, was third in hits with 154, and third in triples with nine.

When the minor-league season was over, Derek, along with minor-league buddy Jorge Posada, was called up to the major leagues. In September, major-league baseball teams are allowed to expand their rosters and most top prospects are called up.

"We were like little kids," Posada recalled. "We kept telling each other, 'Man, this is the big leagues. This is unbelievable. We gotta get here and stay here this time.'"

The two players rented a car together and commuted every day from an inexpensive hotel in New Jersey to Yankee Stadium. The sparse living conditions didn't bother Derek, though. He was in New York to stay. Soon he would be able to live wherever he wanted.

> **When the minor-league season was over, Derek was called up to the major leagues.**

Chapter 6
Rookie of the Year

Derek always proved that he knew the little things that help a team win.

By spring training of 1996, Derek had already proven to the Yankees that he was ready to be their everyday shortstop. The Yankees had a great team, with players like Bernie Williams, Paul O'Neill, and Tino Martinez. They were confident they would be okay with a rookie shortstop in the lineup.

Derek did not play like a rookie. He played like a veteran. He showed that he had great baseball sense, always proving that he knew the little things that help a team win. He knew exactly where to be on every relay throw. He knew when it was appropriate to take a strike and let a base runner steal. He knew when it was appropriate to hit behind a runner and advance the man to second base. Derek proved himself to be a team player.

Derek was the leadoff hitter and helped the Yankees to a first place finish. He was among American League leaders with 148 singles and a .328 average. He even had a 17-game hitting streak.

Derek was unanimously voted the American League Rookie of the Year. Then he batted .361 in the postseason as the Yankees beat the Atlanta Braves in the World Series. Most rookies would have folded under the pressure of playoff baseball, but not Derek. He relished it and became an instant star.

Derek has had many endorsements, including his own breakfast cereal.

Chapter 7
A Perfect Match

New York and Derek Jeter became a perfect mach. He loved the action of the city, and the fans loved him right back. He even made headlines off the baseball field when he dated pop star Mariah Carey.

Even though he is famous and makes a lot of money, Derek himself hasn't changed. His favorite television show is *The Price Is Right,* one of his favorite movies is *Seven,* and he loves snacking on chocolate chip cookies and chocolate ice cream.

Derek has continued to improve his playing since his rookie season, and

Derek has continued to improve his playing since his rookie season.

he has become one of the game's best players. He helped lead the Yankees to another World Series victory in 1998 and another in 1999.

But Derek wants to be even better.

He bought a house near the Yankee training facility in Tampa Bay, and he spends most of his off-season working out with weights or fine-tuning his swing.

"He's the best player I've ever played with and I think a lot of people in the clubhouse are going to say that before he's done," said Yankee teammate Paul O'Neill. "What sets him apart is the number of ways he can affect a game."

Derek is also very charitable. He recently started the Turn 2 Foundation, an organization designed to keep kids from taking drugs. He even hired his father to help run the foundation. Starting a charity was something Derek had

Derek appeared with Mariah Carey at the Puff Daddy birthday gala in New York.

Derek is one of the best shortstops in the Major Leagues.

wanted to do ever since childhood.

Today Derek Jeter is considered one of the three best shortstops in the game, along with his best friend Alex Rodriguez and Nomar Garciaparra. The Yankees realize that and have given Derek a $10 million one-year contract. But one thing is certain: whether Derek is making a nominal wage or millions and millions of dollars, the 6-foot, three-inch right-hander will never allow himself to walk. Derek will always run.

Major League Statistics

YR	TM	G	AB	R	H	2B	3B	HR	RBI	AVG
95	Nya	15	48	5	12	4	1	0	7	.250
96	Nya	157	582	104	183	25	6	10	78	.314
97	Nya	159	654	116	190	31	7	10	70	.291
98	Nya	149	626	127	203	25	8	19	84	.324
99	Nya	158	627	134	219	37	9	24	102	.349
00	Nya	148	503	110	201	31	4	15	73	.330
TOTALS		786	3040	596	1008	153	35	78	414	.310

Chronology

- Born June 26, 1974
- Graduated in 1992 from Kalamazoo Central High School
- Selected by the New York Yankees in the first round of the June 1992 draft
- Named Minor League Player of the Year by *Baseball America* in 1994
- Made his Major League debut on May 29, 1995
- Named the American League Rookie of the Year in 1996
- Won his first World Series ring in 1996
- Named to the American League All Star Game in 1998, 1999
- Led the American League in runs scored in 1998
- Reached base 53 straight games in 1999
- Led American League in hits with 219 in 1999
- Won his second and third World Series rings in 1998 and 1999
- Negotiated one-year $10 million dollar contract with the Yankees in 2000.

Index

Carey, Mariah 28
Groch, Dick 5
Jeter, Charles (father) 9, 11, 15
Jeter, Derek
    birth of 9
    childhood 9-15
    drafted by Yankees 19
    Little League 11
    Major League 19-20, 23-25
    Minor League 19-20, 23-25
    Rookie of the Year 6, 27
    spring training 22
    teenage years 15-17
    World Series 6, 29
Jeter, Dorothy (mother) 9
Jeter, Sharlee (sister) 12-14
Mattingly, Don 21-23
New York Yankees 6, 8, 19, 23-26, 28, 30
Posada, Jorge 25
Turn 2 Foundation 29
Winfield, Dave 11-12, 15